▾ PAIRS ▾

Also by Philip Booth

▼

· P A I R S ·

new poems by
PHILIP BOOTH

penguin poets

PENGUIN BOOKS
Published by the Penguin Group
Penguin Books USA Inc., 375 Hudson Street,
New York, New York 10014, U.S.A.
Penguin Books Ltd, 27 Wrights Lane,
London W8 5TZ, England
Penguin Books Australia Ltd, Ringwood,
Victoria, Australia
Penguin Books Canada Ltd, 10 Alcorn Avenue,
Toronto, Ontario, Canada M4V 3B2
Penguin Books (N.Z.) Ltd, 182-190 Wairau Road,
Auckland 10, New Zealand

Penguin Books Ltd, Registered Offices:
Harmondsworth, Middlesex, England

First published in Penguin Books 1994

1 3 5 7 9 10 8 6 4 2

Copyright © Philip Booth, 1994
All rights reserved

Pages vii and viii constitute an extension of
this copyright page.

LIBRARY OF CONGRESS CATALOGING IN PUBLICATION DATA
Booth, Philip E.
Pairs: new poems/by Philip Booth.
p.   cm.—(Penguin poets)
ISBN 0 14 058724 1
I. Title.
PS3552.O647P35   1994
811'.54—dc20   94–3899

Printed in the United States of America
Set in Garamond #3
Designed by Kathryn Parise

For

TWO
everywhere,
who know love,

their arms
round the griefs of the ages . . .

▼ ACKNOWLEDGMENTS ▼

Thanks to the editors of the journals in which the following poems first appeared, some in versions revised and/or retitled: "Backcountry," "Fog-Talk," "Half-Life," "Room 301" (formerly "Room 310"), "Sentences," "Sixty-Six," "Talk About Walking," *The American Poetry Review*; "Bee," *The Amicus Journal*; "Pairs," *The Atlantic*; "First Night," "First Song," "Seasons," "Seventy," *The Beloit Poetry Journal*; "Again," "All-Night Radio," "Lightly," "Self-Sentence" (formerly "Sentence"), *Denver Quarterly*; "Chances," *The Georgia Review*; "Words," *Grilled Flowers*; "Prepositions" (formerly "Predispositions"), *Kayak*; "First Storm," "Hope," "Terms," and "Waking Early," "Waking Late," and "Reawakening in New England" (previously gathered under the single title "Three Awakenings in New England"), *New England Review*; "Two Letters" (formerly "Letter"), *The New Virginia Review*; "Requiescat: Western Union," *The New Yorker*; "Navigation," *North Dakota Quarterly*; "Sixty-Three," *The Ohio Review*; "Anybody Who Can, Identify Himself" and "He's Half" (formerly "Short" and "Fat" as sections of "Five Figures"), *Ontario Review*; "March Again," "November Sun," "Outlook," *Poetry*; "Alba," *Poetry Northwest*; "Hand," *Princeton University Library Chronicle*; "Looking," *River Styx*; "When I'm : Where You," *The Southern California Anthology*; "Jazz in the Garden," *The Southern Review*; "Worlds," *The Virginia Quarterly Review*; "Linesquall," *The Yale Review*.

▼

"Places Without Names" first appeared in the anthology *After the Storm*, edited by Jay Meek and F. D. Reeve (Maisonneuve Press, 1992); "Sixty," first published in *The Atlantic*, was also part of *Selves* (Viking Penguin, 1990). The epigraph from "Notes Toward a Supreme Fiction," from *The Collected Poems of Wallace Stevens*, copyright 1954 by Wallace Stevens, is here reprinted by kind permission of Alfred A. Knopf, Inc. The seven words italicized in the dedication are from "In My Craft and Sullen Art," by Dylan Thomas, and are here quoted by generous permission of his publisher, New Directions Publishing Corporation.

For insights and challenges which helped shape many of these poems, thanks first and again to Margaret Booth and Patricia Fowler; thanks newly to Jane Mead, Martha Meek, and David Ferry. To Barbara Burn, Chuck Verrill, and Kathryn Harrison, whose splendid editing brought me through previous books, thanks is long overdue; thanks also to Dawn Drzal for her important part in *Pairs*.

▼ CONTENTS ▼

WINTER

▾ PAIRS ▾

Unity is plural and, at minimum, is two.

BUCKMINSTER FULLER

In seed time learn, in harvest teach, in
winter enjoy.

WILLIAM BLAKE

. . . it was not a choice
Between excluding things. It was not a choice

Between, but of. He chose to include the things
That in each other are included, the whole,
The complicate, the amassing harmony.

WALLACE STEVENS

WHEN I'M : WHERE YOU

When I'm writing, as
I'm now writing, I write
from wherever I've ever

been, up through a now
that has no here, out
into a there where

you, in a time beyond
now (to you rearrived
as time present), may

deep in yourself feel
words risen through
me: words no more mine

than now yours, as I
feel how it feels to
write out toward you

our need to figure
all it may mean, in this
very world, to be us.

▾ SEED TIME ▾

FIRST STORM

August loaded with anvil clouds
piled up over Aroostook. Supper,
plump thunder. Over shortcake,

lightning opens the valley
the storm falls down. The barn roof
snares the sleet for a moment,

then rain starts in. The boy
in bed, whose mother closed
the window, uses his thumbnail

to chisel the wallpaper flowers.
The river behind the house keeps
swelling; the boy holds on to

himself, until after. By morning
it looks like October. Looking out
under his shade, the boy can feel

the new weather: his older brother
is already up, outside alone,
playing with his official football.

FIRST SONG

Oh, when the sun goes down,
I want to walk far out from town:
to walk with my love when the sun goes down,
to walk with my love far out from town.

Now when the wind dies down,
I want to lie in the leaves gone brown,
to lie with my love when the wind dies down,
to lie with my love in the leaves gone brown.

And when the stars burn down,
I want to call my love my own:
to call my love when the stars burn down,
to call my love my own, my own.

COME JUNE

Come June, big stars
through cracks in the hayloft roof.

Under rain, the roof
swells tight as the head of a drum.

FIRST NIGHT

Breathing the wonder. Easing
to breathe. Breath by breath, each
with each other: timing the rise,
floating the fall. Together, together,
letting sleep come.
                              Keeping and
keeping, dreaming such sleep.
Sleeping to wake: letting light
wake you, letting the daybreak
hold and behold you, self and
other, together and each.

REQUIESCAT: WESTERN UNION

The yellow pads. The cream walls
and varnished counter. The pencil
on its bright chain: how bluntly

it made the words up, counted them,
then—a quick second blank—
copied them down. Knowing to whom

it was going, how far the sender went
before handing it over: handing it
always to the thin clerk, the man

who figured the cost in his head
before he sat back at his keyboard
to peck out all the emotion.

MR. FROST AND THE MAYOR

Eight years before he died,
at his birthday lunch on
a rich man's island off
the North Shore, surrounded

by early Wyeths and seven
old friends, the duly happy
poet, having used the word
puritan twice in his previous

sentence, was asked by the
single new guest, Joe Grillo,
the Mayor of Gloucester,
imported expressly for this

lifetime occasion, *What
do you mean when you say
Puritan?* Without blinking
an eyelid, or breaking the Mayor's

iambs, the poet cut his old voice
across the question, said *Fear
of man for his own pleasure*
and went on fearlessly talking.

NAVIGATION

Far inland, he
follows the Dipper's
farside pointers
up to Polaris, turns
90° to starboard,
sights down to
Capella, barely
showing above
the low mountains;
his eye, climbing
from there, finds
Cassiopeia, and off
the angled back
of her chair, again
drops to Mirfak,
a dim star in
Perseus, which will,
as the planet re-
volves into dark, give
him his course
to Aldebaran, the
star, if he ever
sails offshore, he
nightly figures
to navigate by.

HE'S HALF

He's half beside himself.
Wanting. Dreading. But he
must love his misery:

he's stayed outside half
his life already, keeping
watch on his inside self,
who keeps saying he's dying
to set himself free.

PREPOSITIONS

The first race he
scratched from,
           a girl
he didn't go out with,
hills he was never
on top of;
          a bet
he refused to take up,
strangers he wouldn't
move toward, leaves he
didn't turn over:
           the boxcar
he didn't climb into,
weathers he failed
to ride out, stars he
still hasn't sailed by,
and poems he couldn't
wake up for;
          poems and
poems he has yet to
work through:
          After, he says,
I get out from under.

ANYBODY WHO CAN, IDENTIFY HIMSELF

The voice is familiar.
I recognize my own hand.
Navel, yes; of a tongue, the end.
Knee, armpit; even, by somewhat
bending, a formerly private part.
None of this is impossible.
But short of mirrors I cannot see
looking myself in the eye.

BEE

A bumbler for sure.
Got caught between the
window and screen. How

he got in, God only.
House as closed to
the world as I've

been all day, numb
to a lot I'm supposed
to love. Didn't do

much this slow day
in mid-Spring, but
needed to free the

old genus *Bombus*.
Took a glass tumbler,
a bent Ace of Hearts:

slipped the glass over
the bee buzzing anger.
Then the card under

to give myself cover.
Took the whole show
to the sideyard door:

at the sill, tipped
the tumbler, then slipped
the card.
        Bee took off
into wavery life.

SELF-SENTENCE

Until he backlit
himself in the glare
of a tall motel window
and let searchlights
probe the unglued
veneer he thought
he'd—up to then—
kept undetectable,

he had all his life
tried to prove to
his friends, to teach
his kids, and demand
of his wife, that every
life is perfectible.

JUDGE

His life, lifelong, denied.
His eyes refused to laugh.
His smile was iron.
Unlocked or locked, his jaw
talked Puritan:

Bad is unforgivable.
Good is not good enough.

LOOKING

Looking for who she
might be the rest of

her life, she found
her face, three or two

new times a day, in
her mirror, trying

to figure how far
the face looking back

at her face might be
from the face she

was looking in with,
a face with more nose

than she liked. She
watched her face with

no makeup on. Giving
herself the eye, she

saw her face wanting
to know if the woman

deep in the glass was
one foot or two feet

away from the *I*
she dreamt to revise,

the *I* she meant to
give back to her life,

once she found some rule
that might measure

how close to herself she
might let herself come.

WORDS

Tears. Tears after all.
I lean over her: *I know,*
I know how you feel.

I lie. It's true:
she's bleeding. She's
readying herself for

dying. Or birth. She's
a child, her own daughter,
the mother she's lost.

She's better. Eased,
I say her her name.
I want to cry. I want

to speak what tears can't.
Emptied, her eyes
reach for mine.

MEASURES

The poems so short.
The life so long to learn.

▾ HARVEST ▾

SENTENCES

Early on, I bought too much
insurance.

         The guy who sold me,
he was thirty, I was twenty-
five, assured me I'd be
reassured. *I was unsure*
all the same, all the same
old Fifties: first the century's,
then mine.

         Some picnic now
I've barely lived to go to,
by a dying farmpond.

The fertilizer's leached.
The old West wind's particulate.
The President's got his bombers out.

Who, at this tail end of centuries,
is fool enough to still believe
he's in control?

         Control of country,
oil, and world: a world of wars
premised on

            no more
World Wars.

         For what we got invested in
—flak-jackets, Scuds, and Bandaids—what
in ourselves did we write off?

         Barely wounded,
uninsurable, in arrears on everything,
including my own gifts,

                              I keep trying to
reconcile accounts: census-counts,
body-counts, and birthdays.
                              What sentences
do we deserve if not the TV views of
Congress, deserts, and dead birds
on which we nightly feed?
                              At gut level,
where we build our lives,

                                        even as we eat
we know we starve.

LIVES

The life we've lived.
The lives we've loved.
Who are we in ourselves?

SEASONS

Bear: beware, from the last days
of August far into November. You
too, you Rails, Gallinules, Snipes;

and from brightest October on, you
Scoters, Eiders, and Old Squaws,
stay clear of blinds and gunboats until

new light lifts you into next year.
And you upland targets for gentlemen
who prefer to shoot rather than hunt,

you alder Woodcock, cornstalk Pheasant,
and deepwoods Grouse, keep your cover
as maples bear gold and go bare; wait out

the sky until the last Canada Goose
has gone over. You, too, you Deer,
spooked for a moon's month in backlots

and hardwood groves grown thick with
riflemen bright with blaze vests. About jack-
lights and treestands there is, in truth,

no truth you will ever know. But you,
Fox and Bobcat: you loners know your times
to lay low, to leave no sign for dogs,

nor tracks in new snow. As for you Crows,
Skunks, Raccoons, you'll soon feel
in what small regard you're held: mere

target-practice for small-bore men, or
boys not yet within range of Rabbits.
Yet after new Christmas guns, even after

the year turns new, it's you, Red Squirrel,
you, quick Coyote and Coydog, and you, slow
Porcupine and old Woodchuck, with whom

I most wish to reason with human reason:
as housewives without blaze vests have fatally
learned, hanging out, like you, in their own

backyards, the laws we keep reinventing
aim for what we most value or value least:
on you, on your kind, who have no reason to know,

the law still says there is No Closed Season.

PLACES WITHOUT NAMES

Ilion: beseiged ten years. Sung hundreds more, then
written down: how force makes corpses out of men.
Men whose spirits were, by war, undone: Salamis,

Shiloh, Crécy. Lives going places gone. Placenames
now, no faces. Sheepmen sent to Passchendaele:
ever after, none could sleep. Barely thirty years:

sons like fathers gone back to the Marne. Gone again to
Argonne Forest, where fathers they could not remember
blew the enemy apart, until they got themselves

dismembered. Sons, too, shot. Bull Run, Malvern Hill:
history tests. Boys who knew left foot from right
never made the grade. No rolls kept. Voices lost,

names on wooden crosses gone to rot. Abroad,
in rivers hard to say, men in living memory
bled their lives out, bodies bloating far downstream.

On Corregidor, an island rock of fortress caves,
tall men surrendered to small men: to each other
none could speak. Lake Ladoga, the Barents Sea, and Attu:

places millhands froze, for hours before they died.
To islands where men burned, papers gave black headlines:
Guadalcanal. Rabaul. Saipan. Iwo. Over which

men like torpedoes flew their lives down into the Pacific.
Tidal beaches. Mountain passes. Holy buildings
older than this country. Cities. Jungle riverbends.

Sealanes old as seawinds. Old villages where,
in some foreign language, country boys got laid.
Around the time the bands start up again, memory

shuts down, each patriot the prisoner of his own flag.
What gene demands old men command young men to die?
The young gone singing to Antietam, Aächen, Anzio.

To Bangladore, the Choisin Reservoir, Dien Bien Phu,
My Lai. Places in the heads of men who have no
mind left. Our fragile idiocy: inflamed five times

a century to take up crossbows, horsepower, warships,
planes, and rocketry. No matter what the weapons,
the dead could not care less. Beyond the homebound wounded

only women, sleepless women, know the holy names:
bed-names, church-names, placenames buried in their
sons' or lovers' heads. Stones without voices,

save the incised name. Poppies, stars, and crosses:
the poverty of history. A wealth of lives. Ours, always
ours: their holy names, these sacrilegious places.

JAZZ IN THE GARDEN

By the summer sea, jazz in the public garden.
Several hundred, come to listen, to watch,
gentle on blankets, sitting among children;
some under trees, a few on the stone wall. One
on a stone bench, come early, her back to the sea,
hearing every note lift, counter, and rise
off the beat. She is fifty; dark, indelible,
her hair cap-cut after chemo, her cheekbones high,
the skin still taut on her dancer's body.
This summer burnt free of pain, she is clear
as the evening: tangible light, sharp calm.
She lives to the drummer's beat: the offbeat
beat of the hi-hat against the bass,
the way his wrists brush the snare, and tip
cymbals. To all else here as remote as Kíev,
she is near to him, close already to being
pure spirit: the shape music takes as the horn
lightly flats its notes and rides on the riff.
It's July by the sea, barely a month past
the solstice. As the jazz closes, lifting to
When the Saints . . . , then letting the people
drift off or begin to talk, she sits on the stone bench,
solo, waiting for him to pack up his traps, knowing
how early the dark has begun to come down.

TWO LETTERS

Acres of feed-corn, rows of it close to
his bedroom window. Stands of longleaf pine.
Home from radiation, a thousand miles
South of where his daughter married to,
he unfolds her letter. Bright green ink
on blue-lined yellow paper.

> *When someone I love*
> *is hurting, I can never*
> *stop myself from wishing*
> *there was something I could*
> *truly do. But when that*
> *someone is you . . .*

He reads that part again;
then, again, he starts:

> *So I only do what I can:*
> *I send my love to you.*
> *Not because I hope that*
> *knowing it's there will*
> *much ease the aloneness*
> *and hurt, but because it is*
> *there, in the heart, asking*
> *to be expressed.*

Out his window, the county he was born to
is all he can see. Miles of longleaf pine
on every horizon his eye can muster. He
knows every field he owns, every furrow
and ditch. Green hundreds of acres,
contour plowed between stands of pine.
He hunted them foot by foot the season
she was born, the years she was little.
He built the ponds he taught her to fish in.
He gave her birthdays worth half

a Duroc, Christmases that cost
beef-critters. And now, by God, it all
comes back. He reads again:

> But when that
> someone is you . . .
> I send my love to you.
> Not because I hope that
> knowing it's there will
> much ease the aloneness
> and hurt, but because it is
> there . . .

He feels it: his big feet under the coverlet
feel for the soil on the Upper Farm,
his eyes fill with the sun that gave him
all he knows to know: the fields between
stands, the seed coming strong in rows
now as far from his hands as her marriage.
It's still there: the growing, the keeping
growing, the turning under, his turning
the tractor to contour the land, to
give the furrow seed. He knows it,

> . . . in the heart, asking
> to be expressed.

Lost in himself, he lets himself feel
the long pain, itself the edge of relief.
He finally finds a pencil, and lets himself go
as far as he ever will. He cannot remember
all their names, his schoolteacher daughter's
daughters; he has never before written them,
but he knows the name of the one
he has never seen, Robin, the spring one.
He tears off the end of his daughter's
long page, and writes in big pencil

> Robbin, I love all
> you girls.

The pain in him rises again, years
of it, more than he'd ever say.
Nothing he'd ever written down
until his daughter's letter came home.
He rests the torn-apart parts, her letter
and his, over the target marks
on his stomach. He looks from his bed
for miles—two miles and far more—
out over pine, back to feed-corn close in.
His eyes sting with tears he still can't let go.

WORLDS

The horizon is flat.
The horizon is round.

Depending, that is,
on the sky's distance.

Depending, always,
on the mind's focus.

Depending on how
one stood, maybe in

third-year German
at Kansas State,

the world is flat
as a Kansas horizon.

Or round as a Kansas
tongue, translating

back into native
dialect all that

Kansas taught it:
Kant, dialectic,

Weltanschauung.
The horizon's often

flat, by degrees
always round. Worlds

depend on the height
of one's eye from

the feet one tries
to keep on the ground.

NOVEMBER SUN

A raw dawn. Hard wind
poured out of the North,
bright whitecaps riding
the Bay all morning,
a new coldfront wedging
through:

        roll after roll
of stratocumulus, come over
a thousand miles of
Canada, unfurling
across the Bay.
Out of the clouds'
flat undersides, over
Belfast and back of
Megunticook, quick
slants of mussel-blue
rain. Slant after slant,
they all evaporate
on the way
down.

        To the Sou'west,
East of Deer Isle, South
of Devil's Head, across
the channel called
Eggemoggin, out into
Jericho Bay, fallen
sunlight keeps falling:
as far as a human eye
can try not to go blind,
the sky is blue beyond
blue, the sea become
hammered gold. Gold
unto gold until,
beyond Whaleback Ledge,
West Halibut Rock and

Saddleback, beyond
the horizon's barely
discernible curve,
there's all the rest,
the spun rest, of
the world.
                   Back here
on Dump Hill, back
in the Town Dump's
Dump Shack, Captain
Durward, now retired
to recycling, Cooler's
boy, and Norwood Caine
and the Mayor of
Hardscrabble, here in
his trademark derby,
snug-up close to the
pot-stove, bemoaning
Perot-votes lost between
here and Texas, calling
by their illegitimate
names every Spotted
Owl freak between
Oregon's Portland
and Maine's.
                   Here, parked
next to the shack, in
the back of an old blue
pickup without any
tailgate, a black part-Lab,
half rolled on her side,
lies in the lee of the
cab, soaking up sun,
November sun. For now,
maybe feeling summer

long gone, she lolls
her head up on the
wheel-well as if she
were Bangor's prime
Animal Rescue League
model: living life
as it's given,

                letting
pure being become her.

BACKCOUNTRY

Fields between woodlots
touched by frost, small ponds
skimmed with black ice. And
Snow apples, bright
on December branches,
hung out over the sudden curve
on a road where a farm
once was.
       I stop to
name them, named not for
the bright of their skin
but the snow inside; you
nod further on to
the mute gold of Russets,
the sky above both of us
blue beyond blue.
              You go
for a Russet, best keeper
of all. I pull down
a Snow, knowing how short
its shelf-life, and hand
it over, bright as Venus
in this month's dawnings.
You trade me the Russet's
sharp meat for the Snow's
veined white, your smile
as low as the solstice sun.
And why not?
           Why are we
traveling if not to slow,
to make our own waystops?
Why here if not to

wake to the planets, name
winter fruit, and harvest,
for once, how history
tastes on each other's lips.

PAIRS

Years now, good days
more than half the year,

they row late afternoons
out through the harbor

to the bell, a couple
with gray hair, an old

green rowboat. Given sun,
their four oars, stroke

by stroke, glint wet,
so far away that even

in light air their
upwind voices barely

carry. No words translate
to us on shore, more

than a mile from where
they pull and feather.

All we hear is how,
like sea-ducks, they

seem constantly to
murmur. And even

after summer's gone,
as they row out or

home, now and again
we hear, we cannot help

but hear, their years
of tidal laughter.

WAS IT

Was it he said she said or
what she said he said?

What

I hate isn't your getting old,
it's your letting me get old.

ROOM 301

Pain. No matter
its source, the trouble is
that it's not abstract: it
embodies theories far beyond
being waved off; it
locates itself, it insists
with a restless authority
that it exists:
                    just as
a big fly, buzzing the room,
tries every last screen,
the night weight of it
—once remote among mountains—
banks in blind, wheels up,
probing for its raw landing strip.

TALK ABOUT WALKING

Where am I going? I'm going
out, out for a walk. I don't
know where except outside.
Outside argument, out beyond
wallpapered walls, outside
wherever it is where nobody
ever imagines. Beyond where
computers circumvent emotion,
where somebody shorted specs
for rivets for airframes on
today's flights. I'm taking off
on my own two feet. I'm going
to clear my head, to watch
mares'-tails instead of TV,
to listen to trees and silence,
to see if I can still breathe.
I'm going to be alone with
myself, to feel how it feels
to embrace what my feet
tell my head, what wind says
in my good ear. I mean to let
myself be embraced, to let go
feeling so centripetally old.
Do I know where I'm going?
I don't. How long or far
I have no idea. No map. I
said I was going to take
a walk. When I'll be back
I'm not going to say.

LINESQUALL

So much upwelling in the sky.
Fair-weather cumulus for hours,
then thickening haze, two states away

from where the front was forecast.
Then this first cell: the cloudwall
building black, topping out at

maybe twenty thousand, in waves
blown sharp as whitecaps. So much
upwelling heat, such updrafts as

charge lightning to let go. Or lift
old tides and farmponds up until,
reformed, they fall back down, given in

to gravity as hail or linesquall rain.
Lightning now; now the first
big drops. We get up, get back in

the truck, still hot. Even with both
sidevents cracked, the windshield fogs;
the downpour blinds the bridge we crossed

to be so stormed. So much fallout from
such quick upwelling. How map our two ways home?
We wait, to calm. There is, for now, no telling.

DANCE

After small rain, the wind
veering into the West.
You gasp and breathe:
I feel as if
I've been walking toward you
all my life.

And I, more slowly, simply
to be here: beholden,
to hold and be held:
I must
have been waiting all my life to
hear what you just told me.

The whole sky, open
to laughter, clearing
to infinite blue:
I know.
For more than half my life
I've been waiting to hold you.

▾ WINTER ▾

TERMS

On land any length of rope that's hitched
to something beyond itself and takes
the strain is called the standing part.
Tossed over a beam or limb, with a slipknot
tied in the farther end, the standing part
could be said to end in a noose. At sea,
put to use, rope changes its name to line.
The part spliced into an eye or, say,
made fast to a shackle, the part that does
the work, that works, remains the standing part.
Any loop or slack curve in the running part
of the line, the part that's not working, becomes
a bight; and the part of the running part
that's let go, or finally eased off
until there's no reserve left, is known
as the bitter end. As it is in other events,
ashore or at sea, that come to the end of the line.

HOPE

Old spirit, in and beyond me,
keep and extend me. Amid strangers,
friends, great trees and big seas breaking,
let love move me. Let me hear the whole music,
see clear, reach deep. Open me to find due words,
that I may shape them to ploughshares of my own making.
After such luck, however late, give me to give to
the oldest dance. . . . Then to good sleep,
and—if it happens—glad waking.

HALF-LIFE

3:00 a.m. Back
from the bathroom,
I've lain awake
for an hour. I
was all right at
2:00, most of me's
still O.K. My feet
are down at the end
of the bed, they and
my head and testicles
still seem to be
the right size. But
my hands, clamped
shut like a baby's
fist, are big as
a catcher's mitt,
each thumb's as big
as a fat man's leg.
I can't get any
sound up from my
throat. I grab
for breath, trying
to cry out.
                    Though
she has been dead
for half my life,
my mother—all
her illnesses
still intact—leans
her softnesses
over my crib,
and tries with-
out words to
hold me. She
tries and tries
to hold me.

ALL-NIGHT RADIO

Barely home from his false-alarm trip
to the local Emergency Room,
the sleepless man, still feeling its pallor,
thinks, abed, from inside his earphones (insofar
as he thinks or listens) that what he hears
is Music Without End:
                                        which is what he believes
the corpse in the nextdoor Viewing Room hears,
the town's most famous swordsman, its last high-roller,
plugged in still, as he always was, to the system
hidden in every high arch of his home-state's
most expensive Full-Service Funeral Parlor.

TOLLS

Midnight tolls its decision:
no one goes free.

OUTLOOK

Lying flat, under a green machine
hung from the ceiling's crossed tracks,
its big crayon-tip aimed at my guts,

I can read its big nameplate: PICKER.
Up from the box the tip comes out of,
three ½" cables, flexibly tied to each other,

climb in long half-loops up a green arm
to the ceiling, before heading out
to wherever they get their power. Which

comes down them into the box, out through
the crayon's nose-cone, through me and
the table I'm flat on, onto film

in a lightproof tray. Two of the cables
look lighter gray than the third. And slightly
kinked, where black marks show the remains

of electrical tape before the advent
of serrated plastic ties. Which now
bind in the dark third, the part

they had to replace to make the whole
machine work: so they could look into
whatever's next, whatever it is I'm in for,

here lying flat as the film that, as
it develops, will show what doesn't appear
out under plain old sky.
                              Sky. Which when I
came in, was just beginning to snow.

MARCH AGAIN

Yesterday the tulip shoots, considering.
Today slight snow on the ground, thin snow in the sky.
Through which, barely, the bronze arctic sun.

The pewtery trunks of old Main Street trees.
The four white chimneys next door, the house
where a woman wrote daily; days like today

she couldn't imagine joys out of doors.
Mine are all locked, no key left. I couldn't
go back in if I wished. And why should I? Twelve,

still, I'm a good ways out on Tunk Lake,
my handline down a black hole in refrozen ice.
Nobody out there but me. The whole surface

uneven, under an incomprehensible sky.
I'm jigging a bright hook for perch, maybe walleye
or hornpout. For whatever I thought might come.

AFTER THE FIRST DEATH

Here's where we live.

At the peninsula end
of the blacktop down
from Bangor. Patchy
snow and bare ground
quilt the old slope
where maybe a hundred
stand at graveside.
Mostly cold.
           He
was our first one.
Like the first boy
who got killed in
Nam, he didn't belong
to any church, he
belonged to the village,
by blood.
           Here we are.
His grandmother, mother,
their husbands, cousins.
Parkas and mackinaws,
women in parkas and
pants, leftover
teenagers shivering
in jeans. Two oldsters
up from Deer Isle
in funeral suits.
A considerable lot
we don't know, from
away. Trench coats,
studded jackets, some
with earrings in
their right ears.
All of us, here,

still fewer than
them buried under
this March hill.
                        We
wait for Carla, the
Universalist minister,
to start. She waits
for the seaducks
in the Back Cove to
quit gabbling. When
they do, she says what
she has to, then what
she wants to. We
laugh and remember,
remember and weep.
                        Now
the final part: Hale,
his red hair flamed to
ashes, gets remaindered
into the ground where
none of his ancestors
speak, where a lot
of his ancestors
lie.
        We back off
and mingle. Some
shake, some hug. Some
don't. Not one of us
walking back out
to the road, our feet
printing the snow,

doesn't know
how Hale loved
where he lived.

The snow's starting
to melt. As we climb
and slip, most of us
watch our steps.
A carpenter, up
ahead, who seldom
speaks ten words
a week, turns back
to me and says *You
read the paper or
watch the news, most
of it feels quite far
from here.*
    Head down,
I nod, and hear
the more:
    *You take
Hale, you take
today,*
   *the world,
you might say, comes
home quite close.*

HAND

In sheer pain, or
desperate to hurt,
it self-clenches;

reshaped to cleave,
tensed hard, it
can strike down.

A child's, taught,
will stretch palm
nearly flat, to give

an apple to a pony.
A man's, wrist back,
palm down, can try

to push self up,
thinking to push
gravity away.

Anyone's, held
naturally, palm
up, cups all

it can't contain:
the frequencies of
light, the weightless

breath of air it
breathes, kinds
of wonder that

the body opens
to embody. It's
true. Hold out

your left, rib-
high, to sky:
feel it fill.

Or know, eyes
closed, it is
already full.

LIGHTLY

The jazz, the beat
it moves to and
across, as you
and I touch, part,

and return to
pulse on feet
lightly lifted,
even as hand

eases hand,
clasps waist or
releases, then spins
as the next riff

floats, plays off
its own low note,
holds to receive,
accept, and then

give, spun by
old returnings
into a new
letting go . . .

WAKING EARLY

3:00 a.m.

    Storm rain come quick
on the dormer, its music
as vital as Bach.

      Reaching
Santayana back to his place
on the headboard shelf,

        I think
for now I feel as peaceful
as Plato maybe felt once.

        Or do
I mean that Greek from Amorgós?
That island poet who knew

         the tides,
who—feeling life's undertow—
loved waking to read, reading
to sleep.

ALBA

A slit of streetlight, angled
on the wall. This side of dream,
waking, I stretch across a time zone to
another state, to you
not yet woken:
                    how your neck
uncovers when your shoulder
wanders, your lips happy
even in sleep; how, displacing
cold, your toes reshape the dark.
The delta and the highlands of
your South, the soft high and
low weight of one breast turning
to the other;
                    as waking, each to
each from there and here, we toward
each other turn, how gentle from how far
your hands:
                    long dear, how deep you reach.

SIXTY

Spring hills, dark contraries:
a glade in a fall valley,
its one flower steeped with sun.

The there and here of her.
The soft where.
The sweet closeness when.

From dreams awake to turn to her.
Remembering, remembering.
And now again. Again.

US

Us. Winter stars.
Measurably far.
Immeasurably close.

SIXTY-THREE

Man I thought I knew well,
feeling his age, asked me
outright, *What do you believe?*

I thought of my daughter
in her hard time, who
learned, between her mouth

and cupped hands, to sound
the prime call of a loon.
I could have said trees,

oaks with fog in them, grown
from split rock next to tides.
I might have said dayrise,

November sun. Or the bow-wave tune
a sailboat plays in light air.
I thought of my daughter

in her hard time; the turn
of the solstice, the way
words find for how life feels.

I know, I said, *without love
there's no music. No music left
to lift hard weathers, to lend*

*old courage its great gift:
to keep believing in love.* From far
in the dark of a lake, the shape

of my daughter's voice got to me:
I told myself *I have to believe.*
Courage takes love and gives love.

CHANCES

As whitecaps ride
mid-ocean swells, and
tumble on themselves,

love's moved to love:
love praises love, proud
of its quick gravity;

love loves to spend its
gifts, gives silence
time, lets hummings

turn to music. Love takes
its chances, touches lightly,
dances to the tune it just

invented. Unannounced,
love pounces on its luck,
lives in eyes alive with

its grave levity. Various
in word, in deed, love,
countless times a day, says

yes. Love knows the names
the other loves, reads
the other's sense of every

tree, cove, sky; in its
fluries, even furies, love's
transformative; while waves

reshape the beaches where they end,
love remains the mystery
love, in us, informs.

WAKING LATE

One settles.
                    Into a chair,
into a lifetime, a life that
falls short.
                    The bulb needs
more watts, the fire wants
more hardwood,
                    But a word
at bedtime, another at
breakfast:
                    one starts
to see the paperwhites flower
in the bowl on the kitchen table.

SIXTY-SIX

Waking himself,

    without any alarm,

after an after-

    lunch nap not a half-

hour before the

    burial service, he

reached for the

    motel note-pad beside

the head of his

    bed to find the six

words, the six

    profound words he was

sure, getting

    up for this afternoon's

interment, he

    had, going to sleep,

written down.

    The words had made beautiful

sense, sense he

    now sensed as terrible

loss, now that

    both he and the words were

beyond whatever

    it was they meant when

they came to him

    from wherever they'd come.

And had now

    gone back to; or altogether

gone out of the

    world in having gone out

of his head. No,

    that wasn't true. Buttoning up

his blue button-

    down, hoisting his pants, tying

his tie in the

those words, all

each other, were,

at home in his

due time, if he

of him, keep his

Rechecking his

again how he

the car, backed

his key to the

to the graveside.

mirror, and combing, he knew that

six, though far from him and

in one form or another, surely

old Unabridged. From which, in

refound two, and could, for the life

mind open, all might come back.

fly, he straightened up, checked

looked, took his flightbag out to

to drop off on the TV top

wordless motel, and drove

REAWAKENING IN NEW ENGLAND

In a house twice older
than I am, a man closing
on seventy, newly
recovered from going
half blind, I'm
home;
             up before
sunup, still dreaming
three women, my back
braced by the grace
of an Eames chair,
I'm here:
             reunited
with Chekhov, living
in books, feeling
for words, revising
this poem;
             here's
where I am, up
against odds,
             having
an ardent dawn.

AGAIN

Now and again,
>   again now
where my body wakes to remember,
I hear myself,
>   like a dog asleep,
return you your sharp small moan.

FOG-TALK

Walking the heaved cement sidewalk down Main Street,
I end up where the town bottoms out: a parking lot
thick with sea-fog. There's Wister, my boyhood friend,

parked on the passenger side of his old Dodge pickup.
He's waiting for Lucia, the girl who drives him around
and feeds him, the one who takes care of him at home.

Wister got married late. Wifeless now, no kids, he's near
sixty-eight. Like me. Watching the ebb, looking out into
the fog. Fog so thick that if you got shingling your roof

you'd shingle three or four courses out onto
the fog before you fell off or sun came. Wister knows
that old joke. Not much else, not any more. His mind drifts

every whichway. When I start over to his old pickup,
he waves to my wave coming toward him, his window half up,
half down. He forgets how to work it. I put my head

up close. *Wister*, I say, *you got your compass with you
to steer her home through this fog?* Wister smiles at me with
all sorts of joy, nodding yes. He says *I don't know.*

SEVENTY

Zero out the kitchen
window. Up 2° from
noon. *Too cold for snow,*

we used to say. The radio
says flurries. Our bones
know better now, our noses

smell the metal sky.
By three, a big low
off the coast; we know

its January weight.
Power lines down. Whorls
of horizontal snow.

At iron dusk, the white-out.
No other house in sight.
Drifted beyond compass,

we light two candles, bank
the woodstove, move up stairs.
In this barely anchored bed

we let our legs warm up
our feet. Which mingled, heat
the rest of us against

the deep old dark. All night
the constant roar: as we once
dove from rocks to swim, we

let old waves wash over us,
waves like this storm,
fetched from a far shore.

▾ ABOUT THE AUTHOR ▾

Born in New Hampshire in 1925, educated at Dartmouth (where Robert Frost was one of his freshman-year teachers), and Columbia, Philip Booth now lives and writes in the Maine house where he grew up. He taught at Wellesley and at Syracuse University, where he was a founder of the graduate Creative Writing Program. *Pairs* is the ninth of his books published by Viking Penguin, following *Selves*, *Relations: Selected Poems 1950–1985*, *Before Sleep*, *Available Light*, *Margins*, *Weathers and Edges*, *The Islanders*, and *Letter from a Distant Land*, the 1956 Lamont Selection of The Academy of American Poets, which in 1983 elected him a Fellow. His work has also been honored by Guggenheim, Rockefeller, and National Endowment fellowships; by Colby College, The Maurice English Prize, and an award from The National Institute of Arts and Letters.

PENGUIN POETS